Ralphi
Rhino

Written and Illustrated by
LISL WEIL

WALKER AND COMPANY
New York

First published in the United States of America
in 1974 by the Walker Publishing Company, Inc.

Published simultaneously in Canada
by Fitzhenry & Whiteside, Limited, Toronto.

Trade ISBN: 0-8027-6176-3
Reinf. ISBN: 0-8027-6177-1

Library of Congress Catalog Card Number: 73-92448

Printed in the United States of America.

10 9 8 7 6 5 4 3 2 1

Big rhinos have strong big horns,
middle-sized rhinos have middle-sized horns,
and small rhinos have small horns.
But what about a very small rhino
that has not yet grown a horn?

"A rhino is as good as his horn,"
Ralphi's father liked to say.

But Ralphi was sad.
He was too small to have a horn.

"As you grow older, you will grow a horn too,"
said his mother.

One day Mother took Alexander,
Bruce, Rhoda, and Ralphi for a ride.
They were going on a picnic.
But Ralphi was still sad.

What fun was a picnic if he had no horn?

Of course Ralphi could not play
"Twirl the Apple."

And Ralphi's brothers and sister did not ask
him to play "Catch the Ring" either.

"I cannot do a thing and no one cares,"
Ralphi thought to himself.

He was so sad that he decided to run away.

Far away.

Soon he saw an elephant.
"I could twirl two apples with his horns,"
Ralphi thought to himself.

Excuse me please.
Could I borrow your horns
while you're resting?"
Ralphi asked politely.

"They're called tusks, my child," the elephant said,
"But you're welcome to borrow them."

After Ralphi thanked the elephant
for his kindness, he admired his new horns.

Then he rushed back to show them off
to Alexander and Bruce and Rhoda.
Ralphi was so happy he wanted to do a somersault.

But then something terrible happened.

The elephant tusks got stuck in the ground.
Ralphi could not get loose by himself.
Everybody laughed. Everybody but Ralphi, that is.

"Sorry to hear about that,"
the kind elephant said when Ralphi
returned his tusks to him.
Just then . . .

Ralphi saw a moose with six strong horns.
Six horns for catching six rings !
So Ralphi asked, "Mr. Moose, could you please
lend me your horns while you are reading?"

"They're called antlers, my boy," Mr. Moose said.
"But you may take them for a little while."

That was fine with Ralphi.
He could not wait to get back to
Alexander, Bruce, and Rhoda.
He hopped along quickly,
not looking where he was going,
when suddenly . . .

he hopped too high!
The antlers caught in
the branches of a big tree.

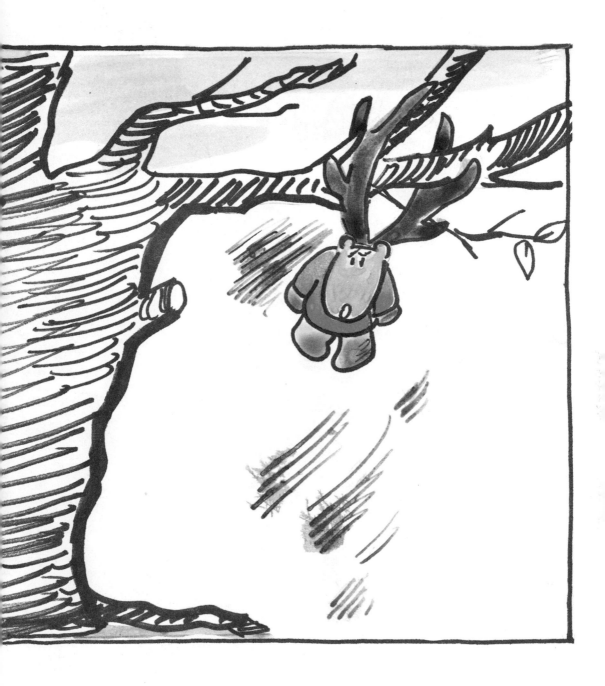

Dangling way up,
Ralphi could not get loose by himself.
"Help, help, help me," he cried.

Luckily
Alexander
and Bruce
and Rhoda
heard Ralphi.
They all
tugged hard
until at last
Ralphi
came loose.

Ralphi fell flat onto his nose.
He got a big scratch that hurt.

But Mother knew just what to do.
"Poor baby," she said and right away she
put a band-aid over Ralphi's scratched nose.

Then they all returned the antlers
to Mr. Moose before going home.

That very night, when all were asleep,
Ralphi felt a little bump under his band-aid.
He tiptoed to the mirror to have a look.

This was no ordinary bump.
Could it be the beginning of a little horn?

Now Ralphi can play
"Twirl the Apple" too.